Austrian Fairytales

Collected from Old Sources

With illustrations
by Lucie Müllerová

Vitalis

Bibliographical Information:

The Giant and the Tailor
From Vienna. Told by a countrywoman from Döbling (now a district of Vienna), this tale was first published by Franz Ziska in Büsching's 'Wöchentliche Nachrichten' (1819) and then in his *Österreichische Volksmärchen* (Vienna 1822, 2nd ed. 1906). In 1843 it was included in the brothers Jacob and Wilhelm Grimm's *Children's and Household Tales [Kinder- und Hausmärchen]* (Vol. I 1812; Vol. II 1815; Vol. III 1822; many editions since then).
Variations on the tale are particularly noted in Styria (cf. Peter Rosegger: *Tannenharz und Fichtennadeln*, Graz/Leipzig 1870).

The Wonder Tree
From Lower Austria. This tale is rare in the German folk tradition. It is taken from Theodor Vernaleken's *Children's and Household Tales* (Vienna 1864, 2nd ed. 1892). Further variations are found in Transylvania and Hungary, as well as in Pomerania.

Wagon "Stick On"
From Upper Austria. This adaptation of the tale told by Eisl, a former miner from Bad Goisern in Upper Austria, is taken from Karl Haiding's *Österreichs Märchenschatz* (Vienna, 1953). It is a variant of *Golden Goose* in Jacob and Wilhelm Grimm's *Children's and Household Tales*. A wagon that 'goes by itself' is also part of the South Slavic oral tradition; the North Germanic tradition tells of a self-driving sleigh.

King Aschelein
From Burgenland. This Animal Bridegroom story was first published in Johann Reinhard Bünker's *Schwänke, Sagen und Märchen in heanzischer Mundart* (Leipzig 1906). It was transcribed in standard German following the dialect of Tobias Kern, a German road sweeper from Sopron in Hungary, who had learnt many old folk tales from his grandfather and friends of his generation. At the beginning of the 19th century, his home city of Sopron was an important northern settlement area for the so-called "Heanzen" (the German-speaking population of southern and central Burgenland), and until the evacuation of the West Hungarian Germans, it maintained close cultural links with modern Burgenland (especially in terms of folk customs, dialect, songs and nursery rhymes).

The Old Grey Horse
From Styria. This variant of the Tristan-fairytale (a type of the so-called steed tale) is taken from Anton Schlossar's *Cultur- und Sittenbilder aus Steiermark* (Graz 1885). There are further variants handed down throughout Styria (the Mürz valley, West Styria), as well as in northern Burgenland and Carinthia. It is also related to the story from Paderborn, *Ferdinand the Faithful and Ferdinand the Unfaithful*, in the Grimm's *Children's and Household Tales*.

The Lost Ball of Twine
From Carinthia. Taken from Franz Franzisci's *Culturstudien über Volksleben, Sitten und Bräuche in Kärnten* (Vienna, 1879). Individual elements are reminiscent of *Mother Holle* in the Brothers Grimm's *Children's and Household Tales*. Further variants are known in Lower Austria and Styria for example.

Mill, Mill, Grind for Me!
From Salzburg. Recorded in Salzburg by Helene Haidinger, first published by K. Haller, *Volksmärchen aus Österreich* (Vienna/Stuttgart/Leipzig n.d. [1915]). Variations on this tale are known all over Austria. It is based on a North Germanic legend where the prophetic warrior maidens Fenja and Menja work a magic mill called Grotti. At first it brings happiness and prosperity, but produces such enormous quantities of salt that the ship sinks and makes the sea salty.

The Bear
From Tyrol. First published in Ignaz Vincenz and Joseph Zingerle's *Kinder- und Hausmärchen aus Süddeutschland*, (Regensburg, 1854). It is a variant of the well-known Hessian tale *The Singing, Springing Lark*, recorded by Jacob and Wilhelm Grimm in the *Children's and Household Tales*.

The Young Count who Travelled in the Underworld
From Vorarlberg. After Adolf Dörler: *Sagen und Märchen aus Vorarlberg*, Zeitschrift für Österreichische Volkskunde 14 (1908). Further variants are known in Austria (Lower Austria and Burgenland) and Scandinavia.

© Vitalis, 2017 • Edited by Harald Salfellner • Illustrated by Lucie Müllerová • Translated from the German by Rachel Ward • Produced in the European Union • ISBN 978-3-89919-148-6 • All rights reserved • www.vitalis-verlag.com

Contents

The Giant and the Tailor

Vienna

A tailor who was good at boasting but bad at paying took it into his head to go out for a while and see something of the world. As soon as ever he could, he left his workshop:

Went on his way
Over bridge and stile
Hither and thither
For many a mile.

Now that he was outside he saw in the blue distance a steep hill, behind which a sky-high tower rose from a wild and dark wood. 'Upon my soul!' cried the tailor, 'what is that?' And as he was pricked fiercely by curiosity, he set off briskly towards it. When he came closer to it, however, his eyes and mouth opened wide for the tower had legs: it sprang over the mountain in one bound and stood before the tailor as a mighty giant. 'What do you want here, you tiny pipsqueak?' he shouted with a voice that echoed around like thunder. The tailor whispered: 'I want to look around and see if I can earn a crust in the forest.' 'If that is your desire' said the giant, 'you can enter into service with me.' 'Well, why not, if it must be so? But what wages will I receive?' 'What wages will you receive?' said the giant. 'I will tell you. Three hundred and sixty-five days a year, and one extra in a leap year. Are you satisfied with that?' 'If you like,' answered the tailor, thinking to himself: 'Well, one must cut his coat according to his cloth. I will soon try to get away again.'

At this, the giant said to him: 'Go, little scoundrel, and fetch me a jug of water.' 'Why not just fetch the well, along with the spring?' asked the braggart, going with the jug to the water. 'What, the well, along with the spring?' the giant, who was something of a dolt and rather silly, muttered into his beard and began to be afraid. 'This fellow knows a thing or two; he has a mandrake in his body. Be on your guard old Hans, this is no servant for you.' When the tailor had brought the water, the giant ordered him to go into the forest and cut a few logs and bring them back home. 'Why not just cut down the whole wood at a stroke:

'What,
All the wood
Both young and old
All it holds
Both knotty and good
And the well along with the spring?'
muttered the credulous giant into his

All the wood
Both young and old
All it holds
Both knotty and good?'
asked the little tailor, going off to cut the wood.

beard, more afraid than ever. 'This fellow knows a thing or two; he has a mandrake in his body. Be on your guard old Hans, this is no servant for you.' When the tailor had brought the wood, the giant ordered him to shoot two or three pigs for his evening meal. 'Why not just bring down a thousand with a single shot and carry them here?' asked the arrogant tailor. 'What?' cried the cowardly giant, considerably shaken. 'That will do for tonight – lie down and rest.' The giant was so terrified that he could not sleep a wink all night for considering how best to rid himself of this accursed sorcerer of a servant, and the sooner the better. Time brings counsel.

The next morning, the giant and the tailor went to a marsh, around which stood a host of willow trees. Then the giant spoke: 'Listen now, tailor, sit down on one of these withies; upon my life, I would be most glad to see if you are able to bend it over.' In a flash the little tailor was sitting on it, holding his breath and making himself heavy, so heavy that the switch bent lower. When, however, he had to draw breath, having unfortunately neglected to put his flat-iron in his pocket, it shot him high into the air, to the giant's great delight, so high that he could no longer be seen. If he has yet to fall to the ground, he must be up there still, hovering around in the air.

The Wonder Tree

Lower Austria

Once upon a time there was a farmer who had three sons; one of them, however, was very stupid, and was thus known as Simple Hansl. He was unsuccessful in everything he undertook and if he tried to catch anything, he would drop it. His father wanted to beat some sense into him and so he thrashed him after each of his foolish antics, but it was all to no avail.

One day, a strange tree grew up out of the earth, without anyone having planted a seed. It grew so quickly that in a few days, it was as tall as a tower, and within a couple of weeks, the top was lost in the clouds. The villagers longed to know how it looked from up there, but for a long time nobody dared to climb the tree.

The people far and wide talked about the tall tree until at last the King's daughter also heard about it, and longed for some fruit from the top. Whoever ventured to climb the tree would be richly rewarded. Whereupon there were many who declared themselves willing to make the attempt but none could successfully accomplish the feat; after two or three days, they all fell to the ground again. They all took several pairs of wooden shoes with them on the long climb; these were intended to be thrown down from time to time as an indication of their progress. Some neither came back nor threw down their shoes. Hansl's brothers also made the attempt but they fared no better than the rest.

Now Simple Hansl himself reported to the palace and demanded twelve pairs of wooden shoes, provisions and a leaden axe for his journey. He set off, entirely unconcerned that everybody was laughing at him. The people waited a day, thinking that he'd soon climb down again. However, they were more than a little amazed when all that came down were his shoes, worn right through. So it went on the next day too, and, as the shoes fell down more heavily, they knew that Hansl was still climbing higher and higher.

So, how was Hansl getting on? He had been climbing for some days when,

one evening, he came across a cave in the tree, from which a light was shimmering. He entered and met an ugly old woman, who gave him a friendly welcome, prepared a good supper for him and offered him a place to sleep. When Hansl had eaten, he asked her how far it was to the tree top. 'My dear Hansl,' she replied, 'you still have a long way to go. I am merely Monday; you must also reach Tuesday and Wednesday, and so on till Saturday, and when you have passed the last, you will see what comes next.'

The next morning, Hansl set off again. Again, he had to climb for several days until he reached a cave. There lived a witch, Tuesday, who was even uglier than Monday, so that at first he was afraid of her. But when she promised him a good supper, he stayed there. In the morning, Tuesday warned him against Wednesday, who was a man who could not look upon human flesh. He followed her advice and did not stop again until he reached Thursday. This was a crookbacked old woman with dishevelled hair and a big red nose. Neither Friday nor Saturday looked any better, but they both received Hansl warmly.

Now Hansl had used up all his shoes and the axe, with which he held fast to the tree, had become quite blunt. He would have dearly loved to stop climbing, but as he didn't want to turn round when he was so far up, he kept going all the same. Soon he came to a stone wall that had grown into the tree trunk. He found a small door, opened it and stepped into a wide meadow. Here he fell down in a daze. When he came to himself again, he was lying in front of a golden city, over which shimmered such a bright light that his eyes simply couldn't bear it. Next to him lay his axe, which now had a golden handle. The top of the tree bore golden fruit and golden animals frolicked in the meadow.

Hansl believed himself to be in heaven and he wanted to stay there. But others say that he climbed down again and told them all about it.

Wagon 'Stick On'

Upper Austria

There was once a King's daughter who was so sullen that she never laughed and there was nothing that could cheer her heart. This concerned her father so much that one day he let it be known that whoever could cheer the mood of his daughter and make her laugh he would recognise as his son-in-law and, some day, the heir to his kingdom.

So, many a nobleman, knight and prince set off to cheer up the King's beautiful daughter and win her hand. But they all laboured in vain when they stepped past the castle, from whose window the girl looked down so sullenly. Whether they sent her up a friendly wave or sought to amuse her with ridiculous pranks, it was all to no avail. However, the King had decreed that whoever failed to bring his daughter round would be thrown in prison for many years.

Thus, when many a suitor ended up languishing in captivity, the others lost the desire to share the same fate and soon it seemed that there would be nobody else willing to gamble his freedom in this way. Then one day a farmer left his solitude to travel to market, where he heard of this strange message; on his return home he related the tale.

His eldest son immediately considered the matter. 'Father, I would like to try it, tomorrow I will set off for the royal city,' and his mother prepared plenty of provisions for his long journey, while his father fetched a shiny silver coin from his chest. The son set off early the next morning. At first he strode forth vigorously, but as he walked for hour after hour through a seemingly endless, gloomy forest, almost all his confidence faded away. When he eventually sought a place to rest, he came to a cave, outside which stood a little old man. 'Good youth, I am terribly hungry, please give me some of your provisions,' begged the old man. 'I need my supplies myself,' replied the wanderer disagreeably, 'it is still a long way to the royal city.'

'You will not make the King's daughter laugh,' declared the old man in reply, and the fellow walked on without a word.

When he came to the city, he went straight to the castle courtyard to try his luck. But the King's daughter looked even crosser than ever, however hard he laboured to cheer her mood as he walked past. So the castle guards seized him and threw him into the deepest dungeon.

Vainly his parents waited a long time for his return. One day, however, the second son said: 'Father, I see that our brother will not return; he has achieved nothing. So I will set forth and win the King's daughter.' The old man was not happy with this. 'Please stay here,' he said, 'you see that it has redounded to your brother's harm; how do you think you will do better than he?' But the middle son stood firm until his parents relented. This time, his mother prepared simpler provisions and his father delved deeply into his purse once again.

The lad set off in good time the next morning and soon reached the forest. He too walked through it for hour after hour without seeing any end and eventually reached the cave, where the little man spoke to him. 'Give me some of your food, I am terribly hungry!' begged the old man, but the lad answered him just as disagreeably as his brother. So the little man spoke: 'You too will fail to make the King's daughter laugh; instead you will suffer need yourself as punishment for your hardheartedness.'

Everything happened as the old man had said. However hard the farmer's son laboured to win the princess round with his carryings-on, it was in vain. The castle guard seized him and cast him into the same dungeon as his brother. Thus they could bewail their misfortune together.

When the second son also failed to return home, the parents became seriously worried. 'Who knows what has befallen them, that they do not come home? And I could do with their help with the work every day; I'm no longer as strong as I once was,' complained the old man.

Now, however, the youngest son also began to grapple with the problem of the King's daughter and one day he said: 'Dear parents, let me also go forth to try my luck! Perhaps I will succeed in winning the princess; that would mean an end to all our suffering.' At first the parents would not hear of it. 'You stay here,' said the father, 'we have already lost two sons who will perhaps never return. How can I manage all the heavy work alone? You might also fail and then we two would be left all alone.'

However, the youngest would not relent; he begged and begged every day until he too was allowed to follow his brothers.

There was no more money for his travels and by this time the supplies were also very scarce. But the youngest set out undaunted and soon reached the little man deep in the woods. He greeted him cheerfully and the old man immediately asked: 'Are you also going to the King's daughter?'

'Yes, dear father, I want to try my luck too.'

'Do you have anything to eat? I have been hungry for many a day now.'

'Certainly, I have bread and bacon. Let us sit here and share it between us!'

So they sat down on two tree stumps and the old man was given all he could possibly eat. When they were both full, the little man spoke to him: 'Because you gave me some of your food, you will also be given something with which I can help you. Here is a little wagon which you will easily be able to pull behind you. If anyone comes up to you and tries to touch the little cart, just say: 'wagon, stick on!' and he won't be able to get away; he'll have to follow everywhere you go.' So the youth thanked him for this strange gift and went on his way.

As he left the forest, he came to a better road and met a chimney sweep, who asked him: 'where are you heading with your cart?'

'To the royal city,' he answered cheerfully, but when the sweep came closer and wanted to touch the cart, he quickly cried 'Wagon, stick on!' Now the sweep couldn't free his hand; it was stuck fast to the cart and so he had to follow, angry and cursing.

As the youngster went on his way with his new companion, he met a baker with a basket of rolls on his back; as he passed, the latter reached out curiously towards the wagon. 'Stick on!' cried the boy quickly and now the baker was running along behind him, next to the chimney sweep.

When he arrived thus in the city, everyone who saw him began to laugh. Then a girl stepped out of a shop; the baker reached for her but the boy called 'Stick on!' and so she had to hang on to the extraordinary vehicle.

So they approached the castle with ever more people running behind him. But when he passed the window from which the princess looked down, she forgot her displeasure and laughed so heartily that her sullen ways were gone forever.

When the King saw this, he ran down the steps in person and embraced the youngest son. He welcomed him, greeted him as his son-in-law and immediately announced the wedding. Then a magnificent coach was sent to the boy's home village to fetch the farmer's family, for the lad insisted that his parents be present.

There was a merry feast and even the two brothers were set free and able to still their hunger at last.

King Aschelein

Burgenland

There was once a King who had a single daughter, who was seventeen years old.

When the King rode out one day, she said to him: 'Father, bring me whatever flies towards your hat.'

The King had ridden for a whole hour and nothing had flown towards him. He rode into the forest and there a bird flew towards his hat. The King caught the bird, wrapped it in his handkerchief and brought it to his daughter.

The girl took the bird in her hand, fetched some wine and washed him in it. She wrapped it in a scrap of silk and in the evening she wrapped it in her quilt.

Every day she gave the little bird food and drink, every day she bathed it in wine and wrapped it in a new scrap of silk. And every night she shared her bed with the little bird.

This went on for a whole year. When the year was up, however, the little bird had changed into a prince over night. The next morning they both went to her parents and she said 'this Prince is the little bird that I tended for a year.'

Although her care had freed him from his enchantment, he could not stay with her for more than three days.

'My dear child,' the Prince said to her on the third day, 'I will not leave you, but I cannot marry you here. My name is King Aschelein. The journey to my country is a year going and a year coming back. If I do not return in two years, I will have died. You can ask for me in my country.'

Then her beloved went forth and she waited long in vain for his return. But when he still did not come she decided to seek him in his country. She took a golden bracelet, a golden comb and a golden carillon and set out on the journey. After a long peregrination, she arrived in his kingdom and sought employment at the castle.

Nobody thought that she was a princess as she was humbly dressed and asking for work. She was taken on as the second maidservant and heard that her beloved had taken a princess of this country for his bride. The wedding was to be on the third day.

So she went to the first maidservant and offered her the golden bracelet in exchange for letting her go to the King's door. 'This is your first day here and you want to go to the King! If you are caught, they will have both our heads.' But the golden bracelet pricked the eye of the parlour maid so much that she let the princess go to the door.

Around midnight, she went to the door and called:

King Aschelein
I washed you with my wine
I wrapped you in my scraps of silk so fine
O, my dearest, chosen child.

Then she ran hastily back to her room. Immediately the King stood up and had his men look to see who it had been. They did not find her, however, for she had long been in her bed feigning sleep.

On the second day she again asked if she could go to the King's door. The parlour maid did not intend to let her, but the golden comb attracted her so strongly that once again the princess was given permission.

At midnight she slipped up to his door again and called:

King Aschelein
I washed you with my wine
I wrapped you in my scraps of silk so fine
O, my dearest, chosen child.

Then she ran away as fast as she could and again he could not find her. On the third day she went to the maidservant again and said: 'I beg you, let me go up to the King's door a third time! I will give you a golden carillon!' Once again, the parlour maid was reluctant at first because she feared the consequences, but she liked the carillon too much and so in the end she said yes.

That night, however, there were four guards stationed in the King's chamber. The princess stepped up to the door once more and called:

King Aschelein
I washed you with my wine
I wrapped you in my scraps of silk so fine
O, my dearest, chosen child.

Then the four guards stormed out of the King's bedroom and before she could get far enough away, they had caught the princess. Light was kindled so that they could see who she was.

'What do you seek by my door these three nights?' he asked angrily. 'I will have you executed.'

'How can you have me executed?' she asked, 'When you spent a whole year resting with me as a bird.'

The King was shocked to the depths of his heart and regretted his harsh words. 'I bathed you in wine and wrapped you in my silken cloths until you regained your human form.'

Then the King took her in his arms and carried her into his chamber. They spent the night together and conferred.

In the morning, the King sent a message to the other princess that he would not marry her for the princess who had freed him from the form of a bird had arrived.

They were married and sent the good tidings to her homeland.

The Old Grey Horse

Styria

There was once a merchant who had a son. When he had grown up, he said to him: 'Here is money for five years and a good steed. Take them, go out and see the world.'

This gratified the cheerful lad considerably. He very soon took his leave of his father, mounted the beautiful horse and rode away with great satisfaction. He had not, however, gone very far when he came to an inn where people were making merry. So he stopped there and gambled and danced so long that he had soon run through all his money and was left with nothing but the horse.

Now, of course, he was no longer joyful and rode on in distress. Then he met a rider on an old grey horse and, because he had no money left at all, he offered an exchange. They changed horses and the merchant's son received an additional five hundred guilders because his horse was so beautiful and he was now receiving an old grey horse.

He mounted the horse, which bore him readily, and rode slowly onwards. It was already getting very dark when he saw something shining on the path. When he stopped and dismounted, he found a golden horseshoe. When he picked it up and took it for himself, however, the grey horse shook his head, as if to say: 'Let it lie!'

However, the youth took no notice of this and rode on. After a little way, he saw something else twinkling on the ground. Again he dismounted and found a golden feather. Although the horse shook his head this time too, he picked it up.

Again they rode on a little way, and again the road shimmered anew. When he dismounted this time, he found a golden ringlet. But when he picked this up too, the grey horse began to speak: 'Do not pick up this ringlet; it will only bring you misfortune and ruin!' However, he was so pleased with the ringlet that he paid no attention to the warning of the horse and took the curl with him.

On his ride, he eventually reached the royal city and, because he now had to earn his living, he entered the service of the

King as a stable hand. There he had to groom the horses and clean the harnesses every day. However, the work had to be finished before dark and it was forbidden on pain of severe punishment to strike a light for it in the evenings. One day though, he had neglected his work and was caught unawares by the darkness. Then he thought of the golden horseshoe, and when he hung it up in the stall, it shone like the brightest light.

However, the King glimpsed the light and immediately had the stable hand brought before him. Furiously he asked him how he dared to work in the stables after dark and to strike a light there against his orders. So the stable hand told him about the golden horseshoe and the King had it fetched straight away. When he saw it, however, he demanded it for himself and threatened the lad with death if he did not hand it over.

It was not long before the stable lad had neglected his work again. In his need he fetched the golden feather. However, this produced such a bright light that it even outshone the horseshoe. Meanwhile, this had not escaped the King's attention, and he had the stable hand brought before him once more. When he heard of the golden feather, the King demanded to see this also, and as soon as he had seen it, he threatened the lad so that he also handed over the precious feather.

However much the stable hand sorrowed over the golden feather and however hard he laboured over the polishing, it happened for a third time that he did not finish his work in daylight. But now, when he fetched out the golden ringlet, it shone as bright as day. The King could not fail to notice this and when he had also taken the ringlet from the youth, his desire increased even more. He called the stable hand to him and said:

'Bring me the horse that shed this golden horseshoe, or else you will be handed over to death!'

Then the lad went sadly back to the stable, not knowing what to do or where to turn. In the last corner, however, stood, almost forgotten, the old grey horse. He stepped up to him now and told him his distress. Thereupon the steed raised his head and said:

'Now you see; why did you not listen to me? But don't be sad. I will help you.'

Now the grey horse told him the way to a castle. There in the stables, next to the noblest of steeds, he would find an old, lame nag. However, that was the one that he must take to the King.

The youth set off immediately, found the right road and came to the castle. There in the stables he met an old, deformed horse that had only three horseshoes. To the left and right stood mighty beasts and he would have much preferred to take one of these to the King, but he remembered the words of the grey horse. He led the old horse out of the stable and mounted it, whereupon it was transformed into the most magnificent steed he had ever seen. He brought it to the King, who at first was overjoyed. Soon however, he was no longer satisfied and called the stable hand to him again:

'Bring me the bird to which this golden feather belongs,' he ordered, 'or it will go badly for you.'

This distressed the lad once more, and he returned to the grey horse to ask for advice.

'Now you see; why did you not listen to me?' he answered. 'But take comfort, I will help you this time too. You must go to the castle once more. There you will see a great golden aviary, in which you will find an old, ugly little bird, more dead than alive, which you must take. All around it will be beautiful, singing birds, but you are not to be concerned with them.'

The youth set forth straight away on his journey and went to the castle again. Amid all the magnificent songbirds he found the old little bird and took it with him. He had hardly left the castle when the ugly little bird was transformed into a fair and beautiful bird with golden feathers. The golden bird sang so sweetly that he quite forgot his journey and was most reluctant to give it to the King.

The latter was extremely pleased when he came face to face with the beautiful creature and heard its song. But soon he demanded to speak to the stable hand again, now ordering that he bring the Princess to whom the golden ringlet belonged. 'If you do not deliver me the Princess on the spot,' he said, 'you are given up to death anyhow.'

Full of care, the lad sought out his grey horse to ask his advice. 'Did I not say that you should not pick up the curl? This is what comes of it. But I will help you,' explained the steed. 'You must go into the castle again, where you will find four rooms through which you must walk. In the first, you will come across a princess of incredible beauty, in the second, one still more beautiful, and the most beautiful of all in the third room. Do not let yourself be tempted by them, however, and go straight into the fourth room. There you will meet an ugly girl with a goitre and a hunched back. This is the one to take to the King.

Again he set off and walked to the castle. When he arrived and entered the first room he met a virgin more beautiful than he had ever seen. In the second room he encountered one far more beautiful still, but the third outshone them both. He would have gladly tarried, but he thought of his faithful grey horse, which had always advised him well, and entered the fourth chamber. Here he found the ugly virgin. He greeted her and led her away with him. But when he stepped outside the castle with her, she became more beautiful and charming than the other three put together, and it was a very bitter duty to have to take her to the King. He received her joyfully and proclaimed her as his bride.

Now the stable hand hoped to have done all he could to win the favour of the King. On the contrary however: the King's jealousy had now been aroused and, even before the wedding had been celebrated, he decreed the lad's death. However, because he had carried out the three tasks so well, he was allowed to choose the method of execution himself and to take three days over it.

Grief-stricken, he came to his grey horse to tell him everything. But even now, the wise animal was able to comfort him and said: 'Tell the King he is to prepare a cauldron, so big that you can ride through it on me. This cauldron is to be filled to the brim with milk and a fire lit under it, so that the milk comes to the boil. Then you are to jump into it with me.' The lad put his trust in his horse and the King agreed to the suggestion.

After three days, the cauldron stood ready in the middle of the castle courtyard and when the milk was bubbling, the stable hand jumped in on his horse. But the horse bore him through it unscathed and when he jumped out with him they were both refreshed and rejuvenated, and the stable hand appeared as the most handsome prince, while his horse was as the most beautiful stallion.

Then the King was utterly consumed by envy and jealousy and, mounted on his steed, he also jumped into the boiling milk. But now both horse and rider sank down and perished most wretchedly.

Now they all chose the handsome youth to be their King but did not begrudge the former king his fate, for he had oppressed them. The young King took the beautiful Princess to be his wife and they celebrated a merry wedding banquet. He always remembered the faithful grey horse and was grateful to him for the rest of his life.

The Lost Ball of Twine

Carinthia

Once upon a time there was a farmer's wife who had two daughters, one of her own and a stepdaughter. Oh, what the poor stepdaughter had to suffer! Even before the sun had risen over the mountains she had to work while her stepsister was still stretched out on the bench in front of the stove.

One day she had to wash some balls of twine; one fell from her hand and the stream carried it away. Full of fear and worry, she hurried after it, but the stream was too fast for her and soon the ball of twine disappeared from her eyes. As she continued thus, suddenly a man with two heads appeared before her. You can imagine how startled she was, but she greeted him politely and asked:

'My dear sir, have you seen a ball of twine?'

The two-headed man replied: 'Dear lass, I have not.' So she continued worriedly along the banks of the stream until, all at once, she met a man and this one had three heads!

'My dear sir, have you seen a ball of twine?' she asked this man too, but again she received the reply: 'Dear lass, I have not.'

So she had to hurry on and after a little while she met a man with four heads, who also could give her no information, then one who had five heads, and this went on until she met a man who had twelve heads! When even he had no knowledge of the ball of twine she became very sad for now night was falling.

Fortunately she now glimpsed a cottage on the banks of the stream, outside which stood a woman. She went up to her and asked: 'My dear ma'am, have you seen a ball of twine?'

'Can you not see that I am fishing it out?' answered the woman.

Then the girl was full of joy at having found the ball of twine and asked for a lodging for the night.

'You can stay,' said the woman. 'What would you like for your supper?'

'Maybe just a little pigswill,' said the girl humbly, but she was given bread and milk.

After she had eaten and thanked her hostess for the food the woman asked: 'Where would you like to sleep?'

'A pigsty is good enough for me,' answered the girl, upon which she was allowed to lie in a feather bed.

When the stepdaughter wanted to set off on her way home in the morning, she had to make another choice for the woman said: 'On what would you like to ride home: a stick or a white horse?' 'A stick is good enough for me,' she responded, upon which she was given a beautiful white horse.

As she rode thus homewards through the forest, a dog began to bark 'Bow wow, golden art thou!' And when she reached her home she was laden with gold from top to bottom.

When the other daughter saw this, she too desired to wash balls of twine and asked her mother to allow it. She hoped to become even more beautiful than her stepsister. The mother had no objection and so the girl went to the stream and threw a ball of twine into the water with all her might, and hurried after it. Like her sister, she came to the many-headed men. She asked one after the other: 'Have you seen a ball of twine?' but none could help her.

Finally she came to the cottage by the stream, outside which stood the woman. When she asked her coarsely: 'Have you seen a ball of twine?' she replied: 'Can you not see that I am fishing it out?'

Now the girl also sought a lodging for the night and was taken in. 'What would you like for your supper?' asked the woman. 'Bread and milk' she answered, but she was given pigswill. 'Where would you like to sleep then?' asked the woman. 'In a feather bed,' she answered, but she had to lie in a pigsty.

In the morning the stepsister wanted to go home, and the woman asked: 'On what would you like to ride home: a stick or a white horse?' She would have liked the steed but was only given a stick. As she rode homewards on it through the forest, she heard a dog barking 'Bow wow, pitch cover thou!'

And when she reached her home she was covered with pitch from top to bottom.

MILL, MILL, GRIND FOR ME!

SALZBURG

There was once a poor widow who had only one son, and he had been abroad for many long years. Although she owned a little house, things went very poorly with her and more than once she sighed: 'Oh, if only he'd come home so I had some help!'

And once as she sat there so, busily spinning with her thoughts far away, all at once the door opened and who should come in but her son. So she cried out: 'I'm so happy that you're back; now things will go better for me!' She also told him how hard and frugal her life was.

'Ah, well we can redress your poverty,' said the son, 'I have brought something back with me.' At that, he pulled a strange bundle from his old, tattered coat, unwrapped it and set an old coffee mill on the table – and that was the entire treasure.

'Oh yes,' said the old woman, disappointedly, 'is that all? My old coffee mill is much better than that.'

'Just wait, little mother,' replied the returned traveller, 'you'll soon see, and do you know what? I'm hungry – quick, put some coffee on for us!'

'I'll do that, but where can I get bread rolls, all the bakers' are shut?' his mother made herself heard.

'That's the least of our worries,' answered the son, 'I'll take care of the rolls.'

The old gammer went out into the kitchen and soon returned with a little pot full of coffee.

'Right,' said the son, 'nobody can see in, can they?'

'We'll just shut the little curtain,' she said, going to the window and pulling the curtain across, a little curious about what would come next. Meanwhile, he had stepped over to the table, began to wind the handle of the old mill saying:

'Mill, mill, grind for me
Fresh rolls by and by!'

He had hardly spoken the last word when the little door on the mill flew open and one roll after another, each as handsome as the last, walked out onto the table. When they had enough he spoke again:

'Mill, mill: that will do
Till I ask for something new!'

Then the little door flew shut again. The old mother clapped her hands in wonder and joy and would have dearly liked to know how it worked. But then her son bade her strictly never to tell anyone what she had just seen and heard or else the mill would be lost forever. She was happy to make the promise and now, with the help of this rare treasure, she was able to improve some things and reach a happy prosperity. She remained as hard-working and God-fearing as ever, did good to the poor and never overreached herself and would probably have continued to live happily on for many years if it hadn't been for a wicked neighbour.

The latter soon noticed that the two souls had better clothes, ate meat almost every day and gave to the poor who came to their door. Because his heart was envious and covetous, he could not rest without knowing whence all this prosperity came. And indeed! One day, the little mother had not properly closed the curtain and when the son said the magic words and the mill obeyed as always, he stood by the window and watched. Now he resolved not to rest until he had taken possession of such a treasure.

He enticed the two good folks into his home, promising them something really wonderful. But when they came, he led them into his cellar and shut them in. Now he ran hastily to their cottage, took the coffee mill and placed it on the table.

Because he was a corn dealer, it came into his mind that he would like to have a great deal of wheat; he turned the handle, saying:

'Mill, mill grind for me
Good wheat by and by!'

And the mill obeyed him too. The little door sprang open once again and the loveliest grains of wheat poured out like a golden stream.

Then the eyes of the wicked neighbour gleamed with covetous joy and he watched at his leisure as the yellow-gold grains streamed endlessly out. It was not long before they were falling off the table onto the floor; and again it was only a short while before the wicked neighbour could wade through them. He imagined nothing wrong and rubbed his hands with glee. It was only when the wheat reached his knees that he became thoughtful. He repeated the little phrase:

'Mill, mill grind for me
Good wheat by and by!'

because he didn't know any better; the mill did its duty and there was wheat, nothing but wheat, until it had almost reached the tabletop. Then all at once the bad man became nervous and he said the magic words louder and louder, thinking that the mill must stop again. He shouted: 'Enough, enough! Mill, mill, stop!' but it didn't stop. Finally he reached for the axe leaning against the stove and struck around him furiously; but, oh horrors! Every piece of the old coffee mill that he had struck off instantly turned into another mill and they all produced wheat, and more wheat. Then the wicked neighbour was lost, for, in a flash, the grains rose up to the window and higher still; nobody heard his cries for help and he suffocated piteously.

When the wheat began to flow out of the front door and through the attic windows the neighbours noticed and investigated what was wrong. They freed the old mother and her son from the cellar and when the son stepped out of the house he immediately realised what must have happened. He spoke:

'Mill, mill: that will do
Till I ask for something new!'

upon which just a few more grains fell out and then it stopped.

When they had cleared away the wheat, they found the covetous neighbour and he was dead. But, because the son had said the words in the other people's hearing, the coffee mill had vanished too. That was nothing to the two good folks though, because what they had put aside lay undisturbed in the cupboards and they lived happily and humbly ever after.

The Bear

Tyrol

A long time ago there lived a merchant who had three daughters. The eldest was kind-hearted but the younger two were proud and malicious and could not stand their eldest sister. Then it came about that there was to be a winter market nearby, which the merchant wanted to visit. As he left, he said to his daughters: 'What shall I bring you home from the market?' Then the younger two demanded new clothes and other luxuries. But the eldest said: 'Dear Father, bring me a rose as a trinket. That is my favourite flower.' But she thought in her heart: 'My father has enough expenses already. A rose will cost him nothing but bring me great joy.'

Now the merchant travelled to the market and did a good deal of business. He bought beautiful clothes and other treasure for his two younger daughters; however he sought in vain for a rose for his eldest child. For they were in the grip of the cold winter and snow lay knee-deep on all the gardens and fields. That was very unwelcome to the merchant.

After he had disposed of his business he set off for home and drove quickly over the ice and snow. When he had already put a good stretch behind him he came to a magnificent castle, which he had never seen before. The beautiful building was surrounded by a lordly garden in which bloomed a multitude of the loveliest roses. So the merchant thought to himself: 'I must look for a rose here as I would also like to bring joy to the heart of my eldest child.'

Thus, he descended from the sleigh, went into the garden and plucked a rose. Then he intended to head straight back to his sleigh and depart thence. However, that was easier said than done. For he had hardly picked the rose when he heard someone calling his name. He looked round in amazement and, to his great horror he saw a shaggy bear growling at him thus: 'You have presumed to break into my garden and steal a rose; you must pay for this. If you send the daughter, for whom you picked the rose, to me here within two weeks the debt will be settled. If you do not, you will see how you and yours will fare.'

The merchant was shocked to such an extent by this unexpected appearance that he beat a hasty retreat. He ran to his sleigh, forced himself into it and drove over the ice and snow to his town. There his three daughters were overjoyed when they saw their father coming. They sprang towards him and welcomed him most joyfully. Soon, however, they noticed that their father was in a very serious and dismal mood and that quite spoilt their pleasure in the beautiful presents. They kept asking him what was wrong until he finally told them what the terrible bear had said to him.

Then the two younger daughters smirked and said to the eldest: 'See what you get for wanting a rose of all things. It serves you right to be the bride of a bear. You don't know how to act around people.'

Thus they taunted her, taking great joy in the misfortune threatening their good sister. But the latter kept her composure and thought: 'the bear can't be as bad as all that.'

She prepared her things, on the fourteenth day she took her leave of her father and sisters, and then drove down the country road until she reached the bear's castle.

He was waiting for her in the garden entrance and gave her a friendly welcome. Then he led her into the lordly castle, offered her refreshments and assigned her the best room to be her residence. There she found everything she could possibly want; she lacked nothing.

So now she lived in the castle and the bear was her companion. She acquiesced in her situation and lived cheerily and happily. But after some time she was seized by the desire to see her father again and eventually she shared her request with the bear. At first he growled and would not hear of a visit to her father. When the girl begged again the bear growled: 'Go where your heart calls you, but you may not stay longer than two days with your kin.'

Then he took a ring from a hidden casket and gave it to the merchant's

daughter with these words: 'If on the evening before your journey you put this ring on your finger, you will find yourself in your father's house the next morning. Stay there for two days. Then in the evening you must put the little ring on again so that on the third day you will be back here.'

At this the merchant's daughter was overjoyed and could hardly wait for evening to come. When it finally grew dark, she put the little ring on her finger with the intention of going to sleep. However, that was easier said than done. She could not rest for sheer joy and it was nearly midnight before her eyes fell shut.

When she awoke the next morning, she found herself in her father's house. She received a friendly welcome from

her kin and her father's joy knew no bounds. There followed a merry day and nobody thought about the leave-taking. The next morning, the daughter who had come from afar said for the first time that she must be back with the bear the following morning. This surprised them all and they persisted so long that the girl eventually decided to spend another day with her father.

It was not until the evening of the third day that she put the little ring on again and fell asleep feeling melancholy.

When she awoke the next morning she was in the castle of the bear. She now stood up with the intention of going to her master and greeting him. But when she reached his room, it was empty. She hunted high and low through the castle but could not find the bear anywhere. This made her very sad, for she had become fond of the good creature, and once again she hunted for him all over the castle.

Eventually she found him lying half-dead beneath the basin of the fountain. She pulled him back, stroked the brown fur and asked him why he was so sad. He answered: 'I thought you were never coming back and I almost despaired.'

When she heard this, she pitied him all the more, stroked him and said: 'Do not give up hope! I will always stay with you and will never leave you again for you are my heart.'

When the bear heard this, he jumped up gladly and cried: 'If I am your heart, you must beat me until the skin flies from my body.' For a long time the girl balked at this, but eventually she agreed to his request. She took a whip and swung it so fiercely that soon scraps of skin flew from the bear. At his request she kept beating so that the whip hissed.

When the skin was almost all flayed away, suddenly an amazingly handsome youth was standing before her. He hurried towards her, embraced her and thanked her for freeing him from the form of the bear. Then he led her back to the castle and they held the merriest wedding.

The servants were also freed from the enchantment along with their master and now the merchant's daughter lived a magnificent life with her husband in the castle.

The Young Count who Travelled in the Underworld

Vorarlberg

Once there was a Count and Countess who lived with their two daughters in joy and prosperity. The only care to disturb their happiness was that they had yet to be granted an heir.

One day an old beggar woman came to the castle and asked for alms. When the old dame had been richly endowed by the Countess she thanked her and said: 'In a year's time you will bear a son and you are to name him Karl.'

This message filled the heart of the noble Countess with joy and she replied: 'That is my husband's name.'

'However, your son may never tread on the bare earth until his seventeenth year, or else he will disappear,' said the old woman, departing.

After a year this prophecy was fulfilled and the Countess bore a baby boy, whom she named Karl. He grew up bright and cheerful, and his parents retained a domestic staff of his own who were to take care that he never trod on the bare earth. Once, when Karl was nearly sixteen years old, the Count and his guests went riding in the forest. Karl followed with two servants who saw to it that he never touched the ground. Then they came to a wonderfully clear forest spring and the Count's son was seized by a violent desire to drink of its waters. The two servants wanted to pass him a full cup but he said: 'I will only stand on the board covering the well, ride on!' But hardly had the two departed when he touched the bare earth in dismounting and vanished. His riderless horse soon caught up the two servants, who immediately turned back but could not find him anywhere.

Karl found himself in the Underworld, quite alone in a vast wasteland. As far as he could see, everything was completely flat and at first he was at a loss. So he wandered all day long, ever onwards, until evening, and still the desolate plain stretched ever out ahead of him. Tiredly he lay down on the earth and soon fell asleep.

When he set forth again the next morning, he finally saw an old farm cottage in the distance. He walked towards it and inside he met a woman whose terrifying appearance shocked him considerably. She gave him a friendly welcome, however, told him to rest and brought him something to eat. Later she asked him if he could also work.

'Ah, of course,' Karl replied, 'I'm young and fit.' 'Then you can stay with us,' replied the peasant woman, 'There is work enough to do.'

When the youth saw her three daughters he was utterly astonished, for he had never set eyes on such beautiful girls in all his life.

But in the evening, when the father of the house returned, he asked angrily: 'What sort of person have you got there? Where did he spring from?' Karl answered that he was the young Count and came from the Overworld. Then the man said: 'Tomorrow you must get up early and mow a large meadow.' The Count's son, who was pleased to have found somewhere to stay, agreed to this and soon went to bed.

The next morning he was ready for work in good time. However, the farmer gave him a wooden scythe with which to mow the meadow. Karl could easily see that he would not get very far with that and set off with a heavy heart. When he arrived at the meadow, he lay down sorrowfully and fell asleep.

At noon, when the youngest of the three sisters brought him something to eat, she found him sleeping. She woke him and asked: 'Why are you not working?'

'I cannot mow with this scythe,' he said sadly. Thereupon the girl spoke: 'Take this and eat in peace. By the time you have eaten, I will have mowed all this grass. But when my father asks you, you must not betray me. You must say that you completed the work yourself.'

Karl was happy to promise this, and he had hardly finished eating before all the hard work was done.

In the evening the farmer came to him in the field and snarled at him: 'Have you finished yet?' He was most astonished that the whole meadow was mowed and took him home for supper. Afterwards, however, the master of the house said: 'Tomorrow you must get up early. There are many fir trees out there in the woods that you must fell by evening.'

The next morning, the farmer gave him a wooden axe. He saw straight away that he would not get very far with that and set off into the wood with a heavy heart. There he lay down and soon fell asleep. At noon the youngest sister woke him again and gave him something to eat. Before he had finished his meal, she had felled the trees.

Karl did not know how to thank the beautiful girl. However, she said: 'If you do not abandon me, I will bring you back to the Overworld.'

'I will never abandon you,' he answered.

Then she spoke: 'Pay attention and be ready early in the morning. When I knock on your door, let us fly.'

In the evening the farmer came and asked crossly: 'Have you finished yet?' He was more than a little astonished when he saw that all the firs were felled and said: 'You can't have done that alone!' But Karl insisted that he had cut all the trees without help.

The beautiful girl dressed before the break of dawn and laid a broom in her bed, which was to answer for her three times. Then she woke Karl and they both hurried away. In the morning, the farmer's wife woke up and went to the door of the room where her youngest daughter usually slept.

'Get up!' she called, knocking on the door.

'Yes,' answered the broom.

After a while, her mother returned and called: 'Get up!'

'Yes,' answered the broom, but not as loudly as the first time.

When the girl still did not come, the mother knocked a third time and told her to get up. The besom answered again, but very quietly this time for the two fugitives were far away by now. Eventually, the mother went into the bedroom to see for herself. There she saw the broom lying in the bed instead of her daughter. Now she knew what had taken place, ran to her husband and cried: 'Get up, quickly, they have both run away! Bring the most beautiful things that you find on the way; that will be the two of them.'

She threw him a pair of shoes, with which he could travel a two-hour journey in a single step. Thus he was soon on the heels of the fleeing couple. But the girl noticed him in time and said to Karl: 'We must transform ourselves quickly; you will be a lily and I will be a rose!'

Now her father came along and saw the two flowers. 'I am to bring the most beautiful things I find,' he said to himself, 'but I'll run another hour first; I can collect the flowers on the way back.' As soon as he had passed by, the girl transformed herself and her companion back into human form and both ran as far as they could. When the pursuer returned, they were gone and he had to go home empty-handed.

When he reached home, his wife asked: 'Didn't you see anything?'

'To be sure I did: two beautiful flowers, a lily and a rose,' he answered.

So she became angry that he had not brought the two of them back and sent him out again. This time she even gave him three-hour-shoes, so that he caught up with the fugitives even sooner. But the girl saw him in good time and said:

'Now we must overcome this last danger. I will become a hermit and you will be his hut!'

Hardly had they been transformed when her father came past and asked: 'Has anybody passed this way?'

'Not a soul,' replied the hermit.

'Then I must go on,' he replied and continued on his way.

So they both resumed their true forms and hurried on. When the man eventually reached home again, he could no longer pursue them for they had reached the Overworld.

The two now arrived in a beech wood, near the Count's castle, and he knew his way well. The beautiful virgin was so tired that she immediately lay down and fell asleep. Karl, however, longed so much for his parents that he did not wait for her to wake up and set off home alone.

When the girl awoke, she found herself alone in the strange forest. Karl was gone and nobody heard her cries. So she tried to find her way out of the wood, where she had no idea which way to go. Eventually she came to a clearing where she saw a farmstead. It was just the time for haymaking, and when she said that there was nothing she liked better than haymaking and mowing, she was taken on.

The new maid went out with the other farmhands to the field. But she was so strong and quick that there was nothing left for the other farmhands and maids to do. So they threw the scythes and rakes away and ran home, saying this couldn't be natural.

But in the evening, when the farmer came home, he said that the young Count had returned and that there was thus great rejoicing at the castle. So she listened attentively and asked the way. The next morning, she asked to be allowed to go and watch the festivities at the castle and set off straight away.

In her pocket she carried five nuts that she had brought with her from the Underworld. When she came near to the castle, she took out two of the nuts and cracked them. Upon this, a carriage emerged, studded with silver and drawn by two black horses. She stepped into the carriage wearing a magnificent dress and drove in dazzling beauty into the castle courtyard. There everyone was amazed by the arrival of this beautiful stranger. When she asked for the young Count, she was led into the castle. In the main corridor, however, an evil enchantment cast transformed her into a ragged, ugly creature. So they shooed such a foul woman away and the gatekeeper was reprimanded for letting her in. But he kept insisting that none other than a beautiful maiden had arrived. The girl, however, hurried to a nearby copse and cracked open the other three nuts. Out came a four-in-hand carriage with coachmen and footmen, all more handsome than you could ever imagine. The girl had become even more beautiful and wore an even more sumptuous dress than before.

As soon as they drove up to the castle, everyone ran over to marvel at such beauty and pomp. The stranger asked for the Count and was led into one of the rooms. Karl entered, but at first he failed to recognise her and asked who she was. Then she answered: 'Do you not remember who helped you at your hour of need?'

Then his eyes were opened. He summoned his parents and cried: 'This is my dear bride, who rescued me from the Underworld.'

Upon this there was much rejoicing and they held their wedding feast.